The Berenstain Bears®
and the
EXCUSE NOTE

Stan & Jan
Berenstain

A GOLDEN BOOK • NEW YORK

Western Publishing Company, Inc., Racine, Wisconsin 53404

Sister Bear liked school. She liked it a lot. But there was one thing about school that she didn't like.

That thing was gym.

Sister liked writing. Writing wasn't easy. But it was sort of fun, and it sure was useful. She could already write little notes to Mama Bear and Papa Bear.

Dear Mama,
I love
you.
Love,
Sister

Dear Papa,
I love
you.
Love,
Sister

She even wrote notes to Brother Bear.

Dear Brother,
Fooey on
you.
Love,
Sister

Sister liked reading, too. Reading wasn't easy. But it was sort of fun, and it sure was useful. She could already read storybooks.

And she knew that if she worked
hard, someday she would be able to
read all the books in the library.

Sister also liked number work.
Number work wasn't easy. But it
was sort of fun, and it was *very*
useful—especially counting.

It was good for counting
sheep to help her fall
asleep, and for counting
jumps when she jumped
rope.

7

But Sister didn't like
gym. Not one little bit.
Every day Teacher Jane
and the class would push
the desks and chairs aside,
and they would have gym.

Teacher Jane would lead
the class in jumping jacks,

GROAN!

deep-knee bends,

OUCH!

and the duck walk.

HELP!

9

Gym was *not* easy. And it was *not* fun! Phooey on jumping jacks, deep-knee bends, and the duck walk! What good were they? All they did was make her hot, sweaty, and sore. Sister wished she did not have to go to gym.

Then one day, as Sister
was getting off the bus, she
slipped and twisted her
ankle.

OOH!

The ankle hurt, and she limped up the front steps. It didn't hurt much, but it made Sister remember something. And it gave her an idea.

What Sister remembered was this:
Once her friend Lizzy broke her arm.
The arm got better, but while it was
hurt, *Lizzy got excused from gym.*

"Why are you limping, my dear?" Mama Bear asked when Sister came in the door.

"I hurt my ankle getting off the bus," Sister said.

"Does it hurt a lot?" asked Mama.

"Yes," said Sister. "A lot."

"Let's put some ice on it to keep the swelling down," said Mama. "And we'll see how it feels in the morning."

15

"My ankle still hurts a lot," said Sister when she limped down to breakfast the next morning.

"You'll need a bandage," said Mama.

"There's something else I'll need," said Sister.

"What's that?" asked Mama as she wrapped a bandage around Sister's ankle.

"An excuse note," Sister said, "to excuse me from gym." 17

This is the note that Sister gave to Teacher Jane when it was time for gym.

Dear Teacher Jane,
Please excuse Sister from gym as she has a sore ankle.
Thank you very much.
Sincerely,
Mama Bear

So while the rest of the class was getting hot, sweaty, and sore doing jumping jacks, deep-knee bends, and the duck walk, Sister Bear just sat and watched.

She was very proud of herself for thinking of the excuse note. She wondered why she hadn't thought of it before. There was just one problem. Her ankle was no longer sore.

So when lunch break came, Sister forgot she was supposed to have a sore ankle. She began to run, jump, and climb with her friends.

Sister wasn't the best runner. But she was a pretty good runner.

Sister wasn't the best jumper. But she was a pretty good jumper.

Sister wasn't the best climber. But she was a pretty good climber.

21

Phew! It was time to take a rest.
While she was resting, something
surprising happened. Someone sailed
a paper airplane toward her. It
landed at her feet.

The someone was Teacher
Jane. She had seen Sister
running, jumping, and
climbing on her "sore" ankle.

When Sister looked at the
paper airplane, she knew
what it was. It was the
excuse note folded into an
airplane.

"I guess your ankle is feeling better," Teacher Jane said.

"Much better, thank you," said Sister.

After school that day,
Sister took off the bandage
and told Mama what had
happened at school.

"Hmm," said Mama.

"I hate that old gym!" said Sister. "It makes me all hot, sweaty, and sore. And it's no use at all!"

"It may make you hot, sweaty, and sore," said Mama. "But gym *is* useful—very useful, indeed. Just as writing, reading, and number work are good for your mind, gym is good for your body. It will help you run, jump, and climb better. And you might as well try to have fun doing it because it's part of school and you have to do it."

Mama was right. Gym still made Sister hot and sweaty, but it didn't make her sore anymore after her muscles got stronger. And it turned out to be sort of fun. Soon Sister got so good at gym that sometimes Teacher Jane let her lead the class in...

jumping jacks,

deep-knee bends,

and the duck walk.